MW01284211

BIBLE KNOCK-KNOCK JOKES FROM THE BACK PEW

written by **Mike Thaler**   illustrated by **Jared Lee**

ZONDER**kidz**

ZONDERVAN.com/
AUTHOR**TRACKER**
follow your favorite authors

To Mary H.
Editor, Friend, & Sister in the Lord.
—M.T.

To cousin, Janice Jordon
—J.L.

TOAD

ZONDERKIDZ

Bible Knock-Knock Jokes from the Back Pew
Copyright © 2010 by Mike Thaler
Illustrations © 2010 by Jared Lee Studio, Inc.

Requests for information should be addressed to:

Zondervan, Grand Rapids, Michigan 49530

Library of Congress Cataloging-in-Publication Data
Thaler, Mike, 1936-
    Bible knock-knocks from the back pew / by Mike Thaler ; illustrated by Jared Lee.
        p. cm. — (Tales from the back pew)
    ISBN 978-0-310-71598-6 (softcover)
    1. Knock-knock jokes. 2. Bible—Juvenile humor. 3. Wit and humor, Juvenile. I. Lee,
Jared D., ill. II. Title.
    PN6231.K55T47 2010
    818'.5402—dc22   2009007395

All Scripture quotations unless otherwise noted are taken from the Holy Bible, *New International Version®, NIV®.* Copyright © 1973, 1978, 1984 by Biblica, Inc.™ Used by permission of Zondervan. All rights reserved worldwide.

Any Internet addresses (websites, blogs, etc.) and telephone numbers printed in this book are offered as a resource. They are not intended in any way to be or imply an endorsement by Zondervan, nor does Zondervan vouch for the content of these sites and numbers for the life of this book.

All rights reserved. No part of this publication may be reproduced, stored in a retrieval system, or transmitted in any form or by any means—electronic, mechanical, photocopy, recording, or any other—except for brief quotations in printed reviews, without the prior permission of the publisher.

Zonderkidz is a trademark of Zondervan.

Editor: Mary Hassinger
Art director: Merit Kathan

Printed in China

11 12 13 14 15 /LPC/ 15 14 13 12 11 10 9 8 7 6 5 4 3 2

SHEEP

Knock, knock!
Who's there?
Moses.
Moses who?
He "Moses" grass once a week.

Knock, knock!
Who's there?
Hosanna.
Hosanna who?
If you want to water the lawn, you need a "Hosanna" sprinkler.

Knock, knock!
Who's there?
Zebedee.
Zebedee who?
"Zebedee" do da,
zip-a-dee-ay,
my, oh, my, what a
wonderful day!

Knock, knock!
Who's there?
Babylon.
Babylon who?
Stop "Babylon;" you're not making any sense.

Knock, knock!
Who's there?
Vashti.
Vashti who?
You should "Vashti" hands before you eat.

Knock, knock!
Who's there?
Eden.
Eden who?
He's Eden up all the candy.

SLOW DOWN!

Knock, knock!
Who's there?
Tobias.
Tobias who?
Are you going "Tobias" lunch?

Knock, knock!
Who's there?
Moabites.
Moabites who?
Don't take any "Moabites" out of my sandwich.

Knock, knock!
Who's there?
King Saul.
King Saul who?
Are the "King Saul"
ironed out?

Knock, knock!
Who's there?
Gethsemane.
Gethsemane who?
We "Gethsemane" calls in one day, it's hard to answer them all.

Knock, knock!
Who's there?
Evil.
Evil who?
Evil grab you if he can.

Knock, knock!
Who's there?
Reverend.
Reverend who?
Will these jokes "reverend"?

Knock, knock!
Who's there?
Divine.
Divine who?
Jesus is "divine," and we are the branches.

Knock, knock!
Who's there?
Savior.
Savior who?
Jesus can "Savior" soul if you let him.

Knock, knock!
Who's there?
Cherub.
Cherub who?
"Cherub," everything's going to be all right.

Knock, knock!
Who's there?
Hosea.
Hosea who?
"Hosea" can you see, by the dawn's early light?

Knock, knock!
Who's there?
Boaz.
Boaz who?
I tie a "Boaz" neat as I can.

Knock, knock!
Who's there?
Bathsheba.
Bathsheba who?
It's Friday night, take your "Bathsheba".

Knock, knock!
Who's there?
Armageddon.
Armageddon who?
**"Armageddon"
tired of knocking
on your door.**

Knock, knock!
Who's there?
Adonai.
Adonai who?
**If you don't let me
in, "Adonai" you
some more.**

Knock, knock!
Who's there?
Micah.
Micah who?
**Don't "Micah"
big deal out of it.**

Knock, knock!
Who's there?
Esau.
Esau who?
When "Esau" his brother Jacob, he forgave him.

Knock, knock!
Who's there?
Yeshua.
Yeshua who?
"Yeshua" I can't come in?

I am! I stand at the door and knock.
- Revelation 3:20 NIV

Pronunciation Key

Aaron—(AIR-uhn) "air in..."

Abinadab—(uh-BIN-uh-dab) "I've been a dab..."

Abyssinia—(a-bə-SI-ne-ə) "I'll be seeing ya..."

Adonai—(ad'oh-NI) "...I'd annoy..."

Ahab—(AY-hab) "I have..."

Armageddon—(ahr'muh-GED-uhn) "I'm a-gettin'..."

Babylon—(BAB-uh-luhn) "...babble on..."

Bathsheba—(bath-SHEE-buh) "...bath, Sheba."

Bildad—(BIL-dad) "...bill Dad."

Boaz—(BOH-az) "...bow as..."

Cherub—(CHER-uhb) "Cheer up..."

Daniel—(DAN-yuhl) "Don't yell..."

Darius—(duh-RI-uhs) "...dare us..."

Divine—(də-VIN) "...duh vine..."

Eden—(EE-duhn) "...eatin'..."

Eliphaz—(EL-uh-faz) "...elf has..."

Esau—(EE-saw) "...he saw..."

Esther—(ES-tuhr) "...asked her..."

Evil—(EE-vuhl) "He will..."

Gethsemane—(geth-SEM-uh-nee) "...get so many..."

Goliath—(gə-LI-əth) "Go lieth..."

Hamen—(HAY-muhn) "Hey, man!"

Hosanna—(hoh-ZA-nuh) "...hose and a..."

Hosea—(hoh-SEE-uh) "Oh, say..."

Isaiah—(ai-ZAY-uh) "I say a..."

Israel—(IZ-ree-uhl) "Is real..."

Israeli—(iz-RAY-lee) "It's really..."

Issachar—(IS-uh-kahr) "...is a car..."

Jehovah—(jih-HOH-vuh) "...you have a..."

Jehovah—(jih-HOH-vuh) "...you over..."

Jezebel—(JEH-zuh-bel') "...just the bell..."

Jezreel—(JEZ-ree-uhl) "...just real..."

King Saul—(KING SAWL) "...kinks all..."

Kishon—(KI-shahn) "...kiss on..."

Luke—(LOOK) "Look..."

Maccabee—(MAK-uh-bee) "...make a bee."

Micah—(MI-kuh) "...make a..."

Moabites—(MO-ab-ait) "...more bites..."

Moses—(MO-zis) "mows his..."

Nehemiah—(nee'(h)uh-MI-uh) "...near my..."

Nephilim—(NEF-uh-lim) "...no film..."

Pastor—(PAS-t r) "...passed her..."

Pentecost—(PEN-tih-kost) "...pen to cost..."

Phineas—(FIN-æe-uhs) "...funniest..."

Psalm—(SAHM) "Some..."

Reverend—(REV-ruhnd) "...ever end?"

Samaria—(suh-MER-ee-uh) "...some area..."

Saul—(SAWL) "...all..."

Savior—(SAV-y r) "...save your..."

Shechem—(SHEE-kem') "...shake 'em"

Tobias—(to-BAI-uhs) "...to buy us..."

Vashti—(VASH-ti) "...wash duh..."

Yeshua—(yay-SHOO-a) "You sure..."

Zacchaeus—(za-KEE-uhs) "The key is..."

Zebedee—(ZEB-uh-dee) "Zippity..."

Zophar—(ZOH-fahr) "so far..."